ELLIS ISLAND

Thomas S. Owens

The Rosen Publishing Group's
PowerKids Press™
New York

Published in 1997 by The Rosen Publishing Group, Inc.
29 East 21st Street, New York, NY 10010

First Edition

Book Design: Danielle Primiceri

Photo Credits: Cover and p. 21 © Ron Chapple/FPG International; p. 4 © Chris Minerva/FPG International; pp. 7, 8, 12, 18 © Photoworld/FPG International; pp. 11, 15 © FPG International; p. 17 © Elliott Varner Smith.

Owens, Tom, 1960–
    Ellis Island / Thomas S. Owens.
       p. cm. — (The Library of American landmarks)
    Includes index.
    Summary: Describes the historical significance and recent restoration of Ellis Island, which served as a point of entrance for millions of immigrants to the United States.
    ISBN 0-8239-5020-4
    1. Ellis Island Immigration Station (New York, NY)—Juvenile literature. 2. Ellis Island Museum—Juvenile literature. [1. Ellis Island Immigration Station (New York, NY)—History. 2. Ellis Island Museum—Emigration and immigration.] I. Title. II. Series.
    JV6484.093 1997
    325.73—dc21
                                                                          97-11538
                                                                          CIP
                                                                            AC

Manufactured in the United States of America

Table of Contents

NEW YORK

CONNECTICUT

PENNSYLVANIA

ELLIS ISLAND

NEW JERSEY

An Island of Many Names

For nearly 60 years, Ellis Island was like a magic door to the United States. Located in New York Bay, the island was first called Gull Island by the Native Americans. It was later named Oyster Island by Dutch settlers. Store owner Samuel Ellis bought the island in the 1770s and named it after himself. Finally, the U.S. government bought Ellis Island in 1808. And in 1892, Ellis Island became the first stop for **immigrants** (IM-ih-grents) hoping to become U.S. **citizens** (SIT-ih-senz). Between 12 and 16 million people passed through Ellis Island on their way to the United States.

◄ Ellis Island was the door through which millions of people entered the United States between 1892 and 1954.

Coming to America

People had been moving to the United States for many years. But during the late 1800s and early 1900s, wars, harsh laws, and bad **economic** (ek-uh-NOM-ik) conditions caused more and more people to leave their homelands. People came from places all over the world, such as Europe, Asia, Africa, South America, and the Middle East. They came to the United States in hopes of finding a better life. But the U.S. government needed a place to **interview** (IN-ter-vyoo) all these immigrants. So, in 1892, the government opened an immigrant station on Ellis Island.

Immigrants who passed through Ellis Island were interviewed ▶ to make sure they were able to work to support themselves.

Welcome to the United States

The first immigrant to go through the center at Ellis Island was fifteen-year-old Annie Moore. She and her two brothers sailed over from Cork, Ireland, in search of brighter futures in the United States. And it seems as though they found them. As soon as Annie got off the boat, a government worker handed her a $10 gold piece. This was the most money she had ever owned.

Over the next 50 years, millions of immigrants followed Annie through the immigration center at Ellis Island.

◀ Like this young woman from eastern Europe, many people came to the United States in search of a better life.

At Ellis Island

Once at Ellis Island, government workers interviewed immigrants to find out if they could earn enough money to live in the United States. Doctors checked each immigrant's health. Only 2 out of every 100 immigrants were refused citizenship. Some immigrants were interviewed for hours. Others had to wait for many days before getting their "papers," or written government **permission** (per-MISH-un), to stay in the United States. But the workers at Ellis Island made sure that everyone was fed and had a place to sleep.

At Ellis Island, each immigrant was given a medical exam to make sure he or she was healthy. ▶

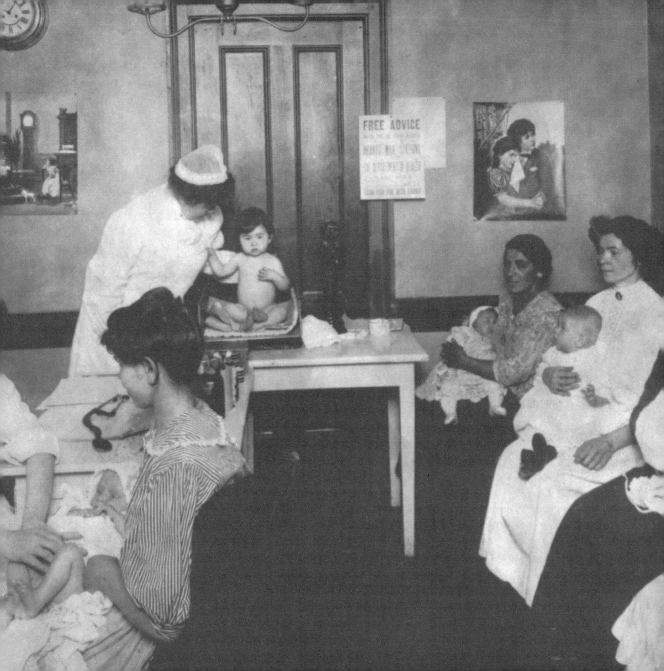

A Taste of America

People from all over the world came together on Ellis Island. In the huge kitchen and dining hall there, some people were surprised by American food. "Some would throw away the banana, thinking it was a core, and would eat only the peel," said Tom Bernardin, a former park ranger and tour guide. "They'd save white bread, thinking it was cake. They only knew the dark, wheat breads they ate at home in Europe."

Tom wrote *The Ellis Island Immigrant Cookbook*, which features recipes that immigrants brought with them to the U.S.

◄ Everyone who passed through Ellis Island was given food to eat and a place to sleep.

High Hopes

Many immigrants heard that Ellis Island was a strange or scary place. Some people called it the "Island of Tears." But people still kept coming. Some joined **relatives** (REL-uh-tivz) who were already in the United States. Others were looking for jobs. Many people heard stories that everyone in the United States was rich. Some people heard that "even the maids have maids!" Many hoped for a country without war. Others looked forward to the freedom to practice any religion. In 1907 alone, over 1.25 million immigrants stopped at Ellis Island to become American citizens.

People from all over the world met at Ellis Island. ▶

Old Fears, New Laws

Some Americans didn't want new people to come to the United States. Many were afraid that **foreign** (FOR-en) people might bring war, take jobs away, or change the country in some way. By 1921, these fears and new laws slowed the number of new-comers to Ellis Island. One of the first laws limited the number of immigrants from China. Then all immigrants had to be able to read English. Soon after that, the government decided on **quotas** (KWOH-tuhz). Quotas allowed only a certain number of immigrants from each country to become U.S. citizens.

People still come to the United States from all over the world. Many hope to become U.S. citizens. ▶

Old Island, New Ways

By 1924, people could apply for American citizenship in the U.S. **embassies** (EM-buh-seez) in their own countries. The **inspections** (in-SPEK-shunz) that once took place at Ellis Island now take place before people travel to the United States. In 1943, the U.S. immigration offices moved from Ellis Island to Manhattan. But Ellis Island stayed open for many years. Soldiers **captured** (KAP-cherd) during World War II were held there. And later, the U.S. Coast Guard trained their service people there. Ellis Island was officially closed in 1954.

◀ The U.S. immigration offices were moved to Manhattan in 1943. This is lower Manhattan around that time.

A Grand Reopening

In 1965, President Lyndon Johnson made Ellis Island part of the Statue of Liberty National **Monument** (MON-yoo-ment). For America's **bicentennial** (by-sen-TEN-ee-ul) in 1976, people were allowed to visit the island. During the Statue of Liberty's 100th birthday celebration in 1986, people gave money to help **restore** (re-STOR) the nearby immigration center. About 140 million dollars were needed to make Ellis Island as good as new. In September 1990, the main building was reopened to the public as the Ellis Island Immigration Museum.

People from all over the United States and the world visit the museum at Ellis Island every year. ▶

Ellis Island Today

Over 4.3 million visitors travel to Ellis Island and the Statue of Liberty every year. Some people touch the "Wall of Honor," which lists over 500,000 names of immigrants who passed through Ellis Island. Others tour the huge museum. Some look at pictures and letters. Others listen to tapes of immigrants telling stories about their time at Ellis Island. More than 100 million people can trace their American beginnings to a family member who immigrated through Ellis Island. Maybe your family's American history started there too.

Glossary

bicentennial (by-sen-TEN-ee-ul) The anniversary of something that happened 200 years ago.

capture (KAP-cher) To take prisoner.

citizen (SIT-ih-sen) A member of a country.

economic (ek-uh-NOM-ik) Having to do with the way a person, group, or country manages its money.

embassy (EM-buh-see) A group of people who represent the government of one country in another country.

foreign (FOR-en) Something or someone from another country.

immigrant (IM-ih-grent) A person who moves to another country to live.

inspection (in-SPEK-shun) When someone looks carefully at another person, place, or thing, checking for certain problems.

interview (IN-ter-vyoo) To ask someone questions about something.

monument (MON-yoo-ment) Something that is built to honor an important person or event.

permission (per-MISH-un) The act of allowing something.

quota (KWOH-tuh) A limited number based on the larger whole.

relative (REL-uh-tiv) A member of a person's family.

restore (re-STOR) To make something as good as new.

Index